WYATT THE MILITARY VETERAN

SUITOR'S CROSSING: THE CALDWELLS #1

HALLIE BENNETT

Copyright © 2025 by Hallie Bennett

Searching for more from Suitor's Crossing?

Check out the *Mountain Men of Suitor's Crossing* series here[1]!

---

1. https://www.amazon.com/dp/B0BZ3F9GG4

PROLOGUE

SIX MONTHS AGO

D*ear Chris,*
        Are we crazy? Because this is blind dating on the next level—communicating through letters when we've never officially met.

Your mom is super sweet (and persistent) and assures me it's not weird or awkward, but I hope you don't feel pressured into anything.

I completely understand if you don't want this to continue past one letter.

Stay safe over there!
Kennedy

K,
        Mom means well. Keep sending letters if you want. It's not like I have much going on out here.
        C

CHAPTER ONE

WYATT LINCOLN

"Dugan, you've got mail." The bright blue envelope stands out in a stack of plain manila, and I can't help but smile at the collection of stickers decorating the correspondence. *You're Great!* stars and *Shine Your Light* suns with goofy grins form a barrage of upbeat phrases that glitter under the fluorescent barracks' lights.

"Thanks." Chris Dugan takes the letter and rips it open without a thought toward the time spent making the outside look special. His eyes scan the unfolded page before shoving the sheet back in its home and tossing it in the trash.

"Whoa, bad news?" It doesn't fit with the letter's peppy charm, but why else would a man throw away a personal letter after a one-minute glance?

Personal correspondence is gold while on deployment.

Our unit has been stationed in this desert hell for months running drill exercises and ensuring we're in top shape for whatever comes our way, so a note from the outside world reminding us of home would boost anyone's spirits.

Except for Dugan's, apparently.

"Nah... It's just some girl my mom wants to set me up with."

"But you're not interested?" I venture, gaze dropping to the discarded letter. My fingers itch to retrieve it.

Thousands of miles away, someone took the time to craft that letter just for Dugan, and he tossed it like leftovers from the canteen. It's not right; it's not fair.

You're just jealous because no one's ever written to you.

Since when has that been an issue? I argue with myself. Plenty of guys get letters and care packages, and it's never stirred up this kind of response. Sure, it's a reminder of my harsh reality—no close friends or family back home after a childhood spent in the foster system—but I've never been tempted to steal a fellow soldier's private mementos.

Until now.

I swear that ripped envelope is practically glowing, the blue paper burning brighter the longer I stare at it.

"She's nice enough but not really my type," Dugan says, breaking the trance the damn letter has on me. "I'll go along with Mom's scheme until enough time passes for me to say I gave Kennedy a fair shot."

"Does she know that's your plan?"

"Are you kidding?" He snorts in disbelief. "My mom has a thing for strays like Kennedy. Shy, quiet, and not much experience with men because of it. I'm doing both of them a favor by going along with the charade."

There's a pop in my jaw from grinding my teeth. Dugan is younger than me and still parties like a new military recruit versus a seasoned veteran, but this seems juvenile—even for him.

"It's your life..." I drawl, forcing my features to remain neutral rather than screwing up in dismay. Out of all the reprimands and warnings going off in my head, it's the least offensive thing to say, and while I'm technically his commanding officer, what Chris does in his downtime is none of my business.

Too bad that doesn't stop me from apprehending his letter the moment he exits the barracks.

I stuff it in my pocket and march to my private room like nothing is out of the ordinary. Like I'm not the creepy motherfucker who is so hard up for *attention, affection?*—I refuse to put a name to it. It's too pathetic—and digs through another man's trash for his scrap of kind words.

Fuck! I scrub a hand down my weathered cheek. *What the hell did I just do?*

CHAPTER TWO

KENNEDY CALDWELL

Three empty chairs surround the square dining table. *Another evening where I feel lonelier than ever.* Technically, I could drive to one of my four brothers' homes for company, but it's not the same as having someone here.

Someone who could have helped me cook dinner.

Someone who *will* help me eat the leftovers, so I'm not stuck eating cheesy chicken and rice for the next week because recipes are not meant for single people.

Even when I cut the ingredients down, I still end up with more food than I can handle before it goes bad. And that's coming from a woman who loves to eat.

"Play a trivia game," I tell the smart speaker on the kitchen counter, shoving my food around the plate with a fork, and a robotic voice starts explaining the rules of the game before asking me a question.

How sad and pathetic is it to substitute a robot for a human?

Desperate measures...

Especially after scrolling social media today and seeing no less than five college acquaintances post about their pregnancies, births, or engagements.

One or two announcements I can handle.

At thirty-one years old, I've been through this cycle multiple times with friends popping out their second or third kids, but to see so many momentous occasions in a row? That got me.

"Marie Antoinette." My answer is correct while the speaker rolls into the next question, and I take a bite of chicken before it gets cold.

If I had exciting news to share, maybe I wouldn't feel so left behind. But my life hasn't changed much in the nine years since graduation and moving back home to Suitor's Crossing to help my brothers run Hearthstone Lodge.

The luxury resort has been in our family for generations—a staple of the town. We offer accommodations for tourists looking to take advantage of the beautiful mountains and hiking trails surrounding us while also providing an upscale space for business retreats, weddings, and anyone else searching for a picturesque setting for their event.

"Tokyo," I say, completing the ten questions and winning the game.

"Do you want to play again?" asks the speaker.

Ignoring the request since it'll shut off on its own, I push away my empty plate and pull the stationary kit I set out earlier closer. My life is routine and boring except for this one bright spot—writing Lieutenant Chris Dugan. His mom, Sheree, attends the same church as our family, and she suggested setting us up on a blind date via letters since he's currently deployed.

I vetoed the idea at first.

What man takes his mother's advice on women?

It felt like an easy way to embarrass myself and get rejected, but Sheree pushed and prodded until I agreed to send one letter to see where things went.

That was a month ago.

Chris responded to my first letter but not the other three. I didn't think a letter a week would be too overwhelming, but his radio silence has me second-guessing myself.

"It's the United States military. Isn't it par for the course that their mailing system is slow?" I mumble to myself.

There are all sorts of legitimate reasons for not hearing back from Chris. He could be too busy doing his job. He could be undercover somewhere communication is limited. His letters could be lost in the millions of parcels that go out every day.

Still, I worry this may be his way of ghosting me from afar, despite the fact that I gave him an out with my first letter.

The thought brings tears to my eyes.

While my friends are enjoying lives full of love with their spouses and children, I'm not even worth the effort of a *'thanks, but no thanks'* letter from a man halfway around the world—a man who literally wrote that there's not much else for him to do except read my letters and write back to me.

Blinking back the waterworks, I force a cheerful tone to my letter.

Maybe this will be the one to encourage a response...

DEAR CHRIS,

I hope you're well! I saw your mom on Sunday, and she's already talking about having you home for the holidays. Sounds like you have a lot to look forward to upon your return to Suitor's Crossing!

The lodge is preparing for a wedding this weekend, so I've been in nonstop communication with vendors and the wedding planner to ensure everything goes off without a hitch.

Do you know Dominic Stone and Avery Monaghan? Avery used to work at Design Time on Main Street. I guess the lodge is special to them because of some event we held here a while back.

It's sweet how we get to be a part of so many people's stories, especially when it results in a happily ever after! Sorry if that sounds mushy, but I am in Suitor's Crossing—a town all about soul mates and heart sparks.

Looking forward to hearing from you. Stay safe!
Kennedy

CHAPTER THREE

WYATT

T*hanks for delivering me! :)*

That's what's written on the back of Dugan's fifth letter. I know it's not meant for me specifically, but it feels like it is.

Because you've been reading Chris's discarded letters, pretending they're for you.

Ignoring the silent jab of my conscience, I study the pretty cursive and smiley face before handing the letter to Dugan. Stickers of woodland creatures decorate the blue envelope this time. There have been positive affirmations, the solar system, flowers, modes of transportation, and now these cute critters. Kennedy must be a teacher or something to have so many stickers on hand.

Or maybe she purchases them special for Chris as a simple way to brighten his day.

A vein throbs in my temple. Dugan doesn't give a rat's ass about Kennedy's letters. Each time he receives one, he rips it open, scans the contents in a quick sweep, then tosses it. And each time, I conjure a reason to hang around long enough to save it from the trash bin without anyone the wiser.

And if I happen to read the letters, too, who's going to berate me for snooping through another soldier's mail? It becomes fair game once it's been thrown away, right?

Keep telling yourself that, stalker.

Thirty seconds after scanning the page, Dugan shoots the balled-up letter in the trash, and just like the past four times, I reach into the bin minutes later and pull out the crumpled paper, waiting to smooth it out until I'm in my room.

As I learn more about Suitor's Crossing, a town that sounds idyllic and too good to be true, the more homesick I become for a life I've never had. One filled with friendly neighbors and quaint traditions versus shuffling between tired foster parents and harried social workers. The only tradition I had was stuffing my meager belongings in a black trash bag before moving on to the next family.

A therapist would probably say that's why I joined the military—I was looking for stability. Structure. A career and life built upon years of traditions.

"Major Lincoln." A private nods as we pass in the hall, and I return his greeting before ducking into my room and sitting at my desk. Flattening my prize over the scuffed wood top, I eagerly pore over Kennedy's latest musings and smile at her enthusiasm about work.

As the event coordinator at her family's lodge, it's obvious how much she loves what she does. She's passionate about people and her town, and it makes me wonder how that would translate into a relationship.

Not that you'll ever know.

Nor will Chris for that matter. He's too busy blowing her off instead of seeing the gem he has right under his nose.

Another wave of frustration crashes through me. I hate that Kennedy is being treated so poorly by him. She doesn't deserve it. No one does.

Placing the letter with the other ones I've saved, my eye catches on the sweet message she left on the envelope again.

Thanks for delivering me! :)

A crazy idea bursts to life as I trace the words.

What if I write Kennedy back?

She opened the door by addressing me first, right?

"Sure, let's go with that," I mutter judgmentally. But I can't shake the thrill of writing to her and potentially getting a response in return.

"Fuck it." Ripping out a sheet of paper from a notebook, I scribble down a quick reply before common sense reminds me why this is a bad idea.

DEAR KENNEDY,

You don't know me, but I saw the 'thank you' note on your letter to Chris, and it made me smile. So I figured I should let you know how much I appreciated the kind gesture since there's not a lot to cheer a guy up out here.

I don't say that to make you feel sorry for me, just to let you know that even the smallest things can have a big impact.

Anyway, I hope the wedding at the lodge goes smoothly. I'm confident you've got everything under control.

Thanks again for your message.

Yours,

Wyatt Lincoln

CHAPTER FOUR

KENNEDY

"**H**ey, Gramps." I bend to kiss my grandpa's leathery cheek.

He peers up through his glasses and grins. "How's it going?" The book of Sudoku he's working on gets set aside in favor of giving me his full attention, and I sink into the sofa next to his favorite recliner.

"Same old, same old." I force a grin, even if contentment is the furthest thing from my mind.

Unfortunately, Gramps has always been able to see through my lies.

"What's going on?" he asks. "You don't seem happy. Is Sheree's son giving you trouble?"

The whole town seems to know about my writing relationship with Chris, except for the fact that he doesn't respond to my letters. You'd think the postal worker tattling about our correspondence would include that tiny detail. Of course, Sheree is another possible culprit—gossiping about her matchmaking skills without the proof to back up her claims of success.

"No, everything is fine. It's just been a stressful week."

"Which is why we do these dinners," Griffen hollers from his place in the kitchen.

He's our grandpa's caretaker, on top of the odd jobs he does at the lodge. It's been four years since Grandma died and Grandpa's arthritis began acting up. Although to be fair to Gramps, he's still fairly independent for an eighty-year-old, but we all feel better knowing someone is here for him in case anything ever happens.

"I know. I know."

Family dinners every Sunday. They're meant to be a time to relax and connect, but these days, the routine is starting to feel monotonous. All of us work hard and don't have much of a personal life to speak of.

Except for Beckett. But what he does in private isn't appropriate for family dinner discussion.

"You're not working too hard are you?" Ezra, ever the observant and protective older sibling, asks from the doorway between the kitchen and living room.

I'm the baby of the family. It's Soren as the oldest, the twins Ezra and Beckett, Griffen, then me. We all work at Hearthstone Lodge in some capacity, minus Beckett. He decided to break from family tradition and became a firefighter instead, which fits his whole bad boy persona.

At least, that's what my friends say.

"No, I'm fine. If I need help, I'll let you know."

I love having a supportive family, but four overprotective brothers is a lot. Maybe it's why I've struggled to date. I've been sheltered for so long that I don't even know how to interact with men outside of my family. And they're all such strong personalities that I naturally melt into the background, happy to remain quiet while they draw everyone else's attention.

The other reason for their overprotectiveness is my health issues. After college, I herniated a disc in my spine, which led to the discovery of scoliosis. Stretches and medication help manage the pain, but my brothers always make sure I'm not overexerting myself.

"Something smells good!" Beckett, Soren, and his daughter Sara Beth file through the cabin door, and our group is complete, meaning it's finally time to eat and stop the inquiry into my life.

Thank god.

Dinner is full of laughter and good food as Beckett shares another wild rescue that his crew was called out for, but my mood quickly nosedives on the quiet drive through town back to my apartment. The silence is such a letdown after a boisterous evening with people who love me.

"I need to get a pet," I say for the thousandth time as I park in front of the triplex. Maybe a cat or dog or even a freaking fish would alleviate some of this loneliness.

Dropping my keys on the kitchen counter, I shuffle through the mail I ignored yesterday since it looked like a bundle of junk—except when I unfold a flyer about a furniture sale, a cream envelope with my name written on it falls out.

An unfamiliar name is scribbled in block letters across the top left corner while 'APO' is listed in the address. *Army Post Office.* My brow wrinkles. If Chris is injured, would they notify me before his mom? Is that even a snail mail type message versus a phone call or an in-person visit?

Flipping the envelope over, I carefully tear the flap open and pull out a blue-lined sheet of paper. Not very official if it's bad news.

"Dear Kennedy," I read aloud, my nerves slowly subsiding as things become clearer. This has nothing to do with Chris, or at least, nothing to do with him being wounded or worse.

Major Wyatt Lincoln delivered my last letter to him, and he saw my impromptu thanks. That's what prompted this unexpected note.

It felt kind of stupid thanking the mail carrier at the time, but now I'm glad I did.

Because it mattered to someone.

Once I reach the end, I immediately reread the letter and contemplate my options. Should I reply? I don't know the man, but if one line on the back of an envelope meant so much to him, how much more would he appreciate a letter?

Biting my lip, I look out the window, enjoying the view of mountains rising on the horizon. Green leaves flutter in the wind as the sun continues to set in an explosion of yellows and oranges.

It's beautiful and serene, but it doesn't answer my questions.

Is it wrong to write Wyatt when I'm also writing Chris? It's not like we're exclusive or officially dating. He hasn't even bothered to respond to my letters.

"But he's reading them..." I realize, connecting the dots between Wyatt's mention of the wedding I wrote to Chris about. How else would he know about that?

Oh, god... Does Chris share my letters with his friends?

I rub the center of my chest where a tightness forms. *Deep breaths, Kennedy. You're alright.* The sound of my large inhale fills the room as I try to remain calm.

Those were private letters. Surely, he wouldn't share them. They're relatively inane—it's not like I'm 'sexting' him through the mail—but they contained details only meant for Chris.

Suddenly, I have to know.

Grabbing my stationary, I settle at the dining table and begin to write.

DEAR WYATT,

I'm glad my note brightened your day, but I have to ask... Does Chris read my letters aloud to your unit? You mentioned a wedding at the lodge, and I wrote about it to Chris in my last letter.

If he does, please let me know, so I can ask him to stop.

It's nothing against you or the rest of your group, but the thought of strangers knowing about my personal life makes me uncomfortable.

Sorry for being so weird. :(

It probably doesn't even make much sense since I'm writing to you—one of those strangers.

Anyway, sorry for rambling. It happens when I'm nervous in conversations, and I guess it spills over into writing, too.

Stay safe!

Kennedy

P.S. Here's an "Awk-wacado" sticker, then "I'll Seed Myself Out".

CHAPTER FIVE

WYATT

A laugh bursts free at the two stickers that fall into my lap. The awkward avocado is cute, but it's the seed strutting through a doorway graphic that gets me. Smiling, I carefully place them back in the envelope and unfold my letter from Kennedy.

I'd hoped.

I'd prayed.

But I didn't really expect to receive a reply from her.

Yet when I handed a letter to Chris—decked out in more fruit and vegetable pun stickers—I found another decorated letter addressed to me. My fingers itched to tear it open immediately, but first, I had to wait for Dugan to abandon his message, save it from the trash, and then retreat for privacy.

Dugan's letter listed more upcoming events in Suitor's Crossing, and the full social calendar for one small town amazed me. Made me yearn for something I've never had. Like fall festivals and community dances.

Then it was time for *my* letter.

I can't help but notice that her words seemed more formal with Chris—focused on facts rather than sharing more about herself—compared to mine, and it causes a moment of happiness before the reason why becomes obvious.

She's worried Dugan uses her letters to entertain the guys.

My stomach plummets, tying itself in knots.

No wonder she kept his letter impersonal. She doesn't want anyone else to read her words, yet I'm snatching them for myself. Invading her privacy.

It's a sickening feeling. One that slicks my gut and causes sweat to dot my forehead.

"Shit," I whisper, stuck in indecision.

I can't stop rescuing her letters from the incinerator, and I can't tell her why they need saving in the first place—because Chris the Jackass throws them in the garbage. So, what the fuck am I going to do?

Save them, but don't read them.

I don't like that option either.

DEAR KENNEDY,

No, Chris doesn't share your letters. I'm sorry for upsetting you with the possibility. He mentioned the wedding in passing, and I stupidly thought I'd send an encouraging word.

Feel free to ramble as much as you want, though I don't want you to feel nervous. As a city boy, the insight into small-town living is a breath of fresh air, especially in this sand pit.

Let's not be strangers...
Name: Wyatt Lincoln
Age: 38
Birthday: August 5
Favorite Movie: Tremors

Favorite Book: ACOTAR—that acronym is a test by the way ;)
Random Fact: I'm an origami master.
Yours,
Wyatt
P.S. I love the stickers. Are you a teacher, too, with this stash?

WYATT,

OMG, that makes me feel better! Sorry I freaked out on you, especially over nothing. It's totally understandable that Chris made an offhand comment.

Suitor's Crossing is the epitome of small towns. I was born and raised here, so I might be biased. ;)

Maybe you can visit one day!

Tremors is a throwback. I remember watching as a kid and being scared, but now that I'm older, giant underground worms are kind of... No, they're still scary LOL.

So, romantasy sunk its teeth in you, too, huh? I think I heard they're making a movie or something based on that series.

An origami master? I'm intrigued. What can you make?

Alright, let's be friends...

Name: Kennedy Caldwell
Age: 31
Birthday: March 17
Favorite Movie: Austenland
Favorite Book: TDWKTM (You're not gonna guess this, but I had to do an acronym, too!)
Random Fact: I can list all 50 states in alphabetical order.
Please be careful in that 'sand pit',
Kennedy

P.S. Nope, not a teacher! I just love stickers, so I'm a bit of a collector/hoarder.

KENNEDY,

*Adding a visit to Suitor's Crossing to my bucket list. Any suggestions for what a tourist should see?

Hmm... I'm sensing we may have different tastes in entertainment. And as hard as I tried, I couldn't break the code of your favorite book. I'm officially stumped.

My origami specialty is a classic—the swan. An art teacher taught us in class one day, and I was hooked. I checked out an origami book from the library to memorize all the ways I could fold squares of paper into animals, flowers, you name it.

There are worse things you could hoard... Toenails, teeth, used bandaids... Stickers seem like a wise choice when you think about it.

Yours,

Wyatt

P.S. In case you don't hear from me, my number is below, if you want to text. No pressure! I just don't want you to worry if a letter gets lost in the mail and weeks go by in radio silence.

CHAPTER SIX

KENNEDY

"W hat's got you smiling?" Beth asks from my office doorway.

I knew I should have shut the door.

Flipping my phone over as if I'm not guilty of texting during work hours, I lie, "Nothing. Just a meme," and cross my fingers under my desk.

Beth moved to town a month ago after her friend Caroline suggested she apply for a job at city hall. Apparently, Beth wanted a change—and most of her friends now live in Suitor's Crossing—so she took the plunge.

I admire her courage, and we hit it off immediately during a meeting to discuss Hearthstone Lodge hosting a city hall event.

"A meme?" Beth's forehead crinkles in doubt. "That's the same moony-eyed look Caroline gets whenever Snow is around."

"I'm not moony-eyed, and our coffee date isn't for another fifteen minutes. You're early." *Diverting the conversation is always a good tactic, right?*

"Good thing, too, or else you'd still be keeping secrets from me, so spill. What's going on? Did Chris finally start making an effort for you?"

All of my friends know about the Ghosting of Chris Dugan. He still hasn't acknowledged my letters, which honestly is a dick move—something I'll never say to Sheree. She thinks the sun shines out of his ass, especially with the whole 'military' thing.

Frustration boils to the forefront again at the reminder of Chris's bad behavior, and I'll take anger over sadness any day. His rejection would have decimated me to tears a few months ago, but Wyatt's correspondence eases the pain.

Because he actually replies, and not just in letters.

We've been texting since he sent his phone number—hence my smile earlier—and our conversations are easy. Comforting. Probably because he's thousands of miles away and doesn't have to deal with my brothers or my awkwardness up close and personal.

There's a barrier between us. One that invites vulnerability rather than my usual shyness.

"It's not Chris." I close out the tabs on my desktop screen then stretch before grabbing my purse.

"Then who is it? One of Beckett's hot firefighter friends? Or a business associate of Ezra's?" Excitement magnifies in Beth's pupils. "Oh, let it be that one! Talk about a taboo pairing. Your brother would freak."

Beth hasn't met all of my family yet, but she's heard rumors about the Suitor's Crossing bad boy, Beckett Caldwell, and knows Ezra mingles in an international crowd with his elite financial group.

"Nope." We walk to the lodge's exclusive coffee shop and order our drinks before meandering out to the brick patio that overlooks the mountains and forests surrounding a glittering lake. We usually mix up our meetings between Hearthstone's coffee and Crossing's Cups & Cakes in town, and today is a lodge day.

"Is it any of your brothers' friends?" she asks. Our metal chairs scrape across the bricks as we settle in for an afternoon chat.

I shake my head, hiding a smile behind my iced coffee.

Beth taps a finger against her lips. "Mysterious... A stranger."

"Well, he knows someone I know."

"A friend of a friend. God, I wish my friends hooked me up like that. Motorcycle men galore and not a one for me." She sighs, referencing the Reaper's Wolves MC—a local motorcycle club chock full of military veterans, some who are also in relationships with several of her book club friends.

Taking pity on her, because really, it's not like Chris intentionally set me and Wyatt up, I admit, "It's someone in Chris's unit. I wrote a silly note of gratitude on the back of an envelope addressed to Chris, and Wyatt replied. The responsibility of throwing us together really lies with fate, not a generous friend."

"Ah, fate. *Heart sparks.*"

I blush at the mention of the legend of love. An old bridge rests at the edge of Suitor's Crossing, though a replica welcomes new visitors on the other side of town, and there's a widely believed story about a town founder crossing the bridge with the girl he was courting and being struck by the knowledge that she was his soul mate. His *heart spark*.

I've heard the story since I was a little girl, and I've dreamed of experiencing the magic myself, but nothing has ever come close to the feeling.

Except for now.

It hasn't occurred to me before, but could Wyatt be my *heart spark*?

We certainly have a connection even though we've never talked in person. Or met in real life. Or have *plans* to meet.

Which is really the issue.

What can happen between two people with half a world between them?

WYATT,

I've included a pamphlet from the Suitor's Crossing Visitor's Center and highlighted the 'must-see' places if you're ever in town. Notice how I even marked Hearthstone Lodge as a place to visit... ;)

As far as code-breaking, it's obvious I possess superior skills LOL. The acronym stands for The Duke Who Knew Too Much. It's a historical romance novel by one of my favorite authors, Grace Callaway.

Speaking of favorite things...

Wow! What an impact that art teacher had on you; I'm sure your parents appreciated your interest in something outside of video games (my brothers were obsessed with our PlayStation growing up, though I was addicted to Crash Bandicoot, too).

I kind of wish I'd thought to explore other sections of the library. Finding an origami book was smart! Who knows what I could have learned if I'd ventured past the fiction section?

Also, thank you for supporting my sticker addiction. You're right. It could be worse. (I'll just keep my jars of hair trimmings a secret...)

In other news, the lodge's van crapped out on me while hauling our set-up for Apple Fest, so I got to spend an afternoon in Dusty's waiting room, which wasn't so bad since their receptionist, Faith, had her baby with her. He's so cute! And squishy.

And... you probably don't care to hear about a stranger's baby.

I'm going to take this as my cue to wrap up LOL.

Talk to you soon, and stay safe!

Kennedy

KENNEDY,

Thanks for the brochure. Suitor's Crossing looks as beautiful as I imagined.

I never knew my parents. I was dropped off at a firehouse at three days old, so my life revolved around the foster system. None of those families cared what I did—video games, origami, or staying out late at skate parks. But don't feel too sorry for me, it wasn't a terrible life, just an adventurous one.

When a friend of mine aged out at eighteen and then joined the military, it seemed natural to follow in his footsteps after high school graduation. There's actually a lot of overlap between the army and foster care. Although I have more structure now, I still move around a lot and meet a ton of new people.

Some day, it might be nice to settle down and place roots in a place where they have time to grow...

Yours,

Wyatt

P.S. Here's an origami swan. It mails well since it lays flat before the last step—inflation—which is where you blow into the hole at the bottom to fill out its body.

P.P.S. Yes, I realize how that sounds LOL.

P.P.P.S. Are three post-scripts a thing? I'm glad you were safe despite car trouble, and I'm happy to read/listen to whatever you want to tell me—babies included.

KENNEDY: **sends a GIF of a penguin waving 'Hello'** Our first text exchange. Hopefully, this is okay...

Wyatt: **a picture of 'Hello' written in the sand** More than okay! :) What's on your agenda today?

Kennedy: We're hosting homecoming parties for the high school's 10th, 25th, and 50th reunions this weekend, so there's a lot of prep work being done. I'm also babysitting my niece's bunny. Look how cute he is! **picture of white bunny chewing a carrot**

Wyatt: You're adorable, and so is that bunny. What's his name?

Kennedy: Whiskers :D I've been thinking about getting a pet, but I'm not sure.

Wyatt: What's holding you back? I always wanted a dog... Thankfully, now I get to hang out with our K9 companions when they're off duty. **picture of a Belgian Malinois** This is Rex.

Kennedy: **heart eyes emoji** I'm so jealous! Honestly, I psych myself out with how much responsibility it is. A lifetime commitment, you know? And generally, I don't shy away from responsibilities or commitments, but I worry about not being able to give a pet its best life. Maybe it's because I don't have a lot of experience. We didn't grow up with pets. Our parents always said five kids was enough.

Wyatt: Don't sell yourself short. You can conquer anything you put your mind to, including pet parenthood. I mean you're juggling three major parties this weekend like a pro, and this is just one of the many events you organize. You're a fucking rockstar, Kennedy.

Kennedy: ...

Kennedy: Thank you *blushing emoji*

Kennedy: Speaking of rockstars, or at least celebrities... Celebrity-adjacent? You'll never guess who just made reservations to stay at the lodge...

CHAPTER SEVEN

WYATT

B efore Kennedy, I planned on re-enlisting.

Now there's someone waiting for me outside of the army, or I hope that's the case. It's taken me a few weeks to get everything sorted, but I'm officially free of my military obligations and driving across the bridge welcoming me to Suitor's Crossing.

Kennedy isn't expecting me, and a frisson of worry seeps into my mind.

We've exchanged letters and text messages for months, so it's not like we're strangers anymore, but there's still a level of anonymity between us—one I'll be demolishing with this visit.

Is this too soon?

Will I scare Kennedy away by visiting without warning?

Questioning the wisdom of my plan, I park along a gravel road where other trucks and sedans are. Kennedy texted earlier about how eager she was to help her friends set up Holiday Lane, a light tour through the forest for town residents and visitors alike.

I figured meeting her in front of a crowd of trusted friends might be better than appearing at her doorstep, so that's why

I asked the gas station attendant on my way into town where Holiday Lane was located and made my way here.

People eye my rental suspiciously, and as soon as I exit the SUV, a large man approaches.

"Everything okay? Are you having car trouble?"

"Not exactly. I'm here to see Kennedy."

The man's brows raise to his hairline as he jerks to a stop. "Kennedy Caldwell?"

"Yeah, this is kind of a surprise." I shrug but stand tall. I'm here for my girl. Determined to meet the woman I've been falling for since her first letter.

"Okay..." he drawls, his eyes narrowing. "Follow me."

We pass the group watching us curiously, until we run into three women stringing lights between painted PVC pipes.

"Kennedy, you have a visitor."

"What?" The brunette in a knitted beanie glances up from detangling a bundle of lights, and my breath seizes in my lungs.

Damn, she's gorgeous.

We never exchanged photos of ourselves, despite adding text messages to our correspondence. I might have been desperate to put a face to the humorous anecdotes and sweetly sincere insights Kennedy wrote, but I didn't want to make her uncomfortable, so I kept the desire to myself.

Stepping forward, I wave her letters in the air—they're my insurance that I am who I say I am.

"It's me. Wyatt. You said I should visit Suitor's Crossing, and Christmas seemed as good a time as any." I inject as much lightheartedness as I can muster while I wait for her response.

Maybe I should have inserted myself into Dugan's holiday plans and returned home with him. He has leave this year, and it would have been easy enough to drop a few hints here and there to garner an invite.

Except I didn't want to rely on Dugan.

Especially when I'm not one hundred percent sure of where he and Kennedy stand. She continued to send him letters, though they became infrequent compared to mine.

"Wyatt? Oh my god!" Kennedy rushes forward and throws her arms around me in a hug full of warmth and the sugary scent of her shampoo, before she quickly retreats. "Sorry, I didn't mean to attack you." A blush deepens the red of her already rosy cheeks.

"Don't apologize." My voice drops lower, so our conversation remains private. "It's been a long time since I've been hugged, and there's a backlog I'd be happy to give you."

Truthfully, hugs have never been my thing. Physical affection in general has been few and far between, so if I'm a bit touch-starved, Kennedy is the woman I want to remedy the problem.

Maybe this wasn't such a terrible idea, after all.

CHAPTER EIGHT

KENNEDY

W*yatt is here.*
In Suitor's Crossing.

Because of *me.*

A volcano of giddiness pulses through my veins, but I try to rein it in. It's bad enough I already jumped the poor man with my overexcited hug.

Motioning to the side to put space between us and the contingent of volunteers curious to know what's going on, I ask, "Why didn't you tell me you were coming? We could have met in town instead of you trekking out to the middle of the woods."

"It's not the worst place I've ever trekked," he says with a grin. "I wanted to surprise you. Is that okay?"

Okay? It's the most romantic thing anyone has ever done for me.

Can it be romantic if our conversations never ventured past playful flirting?

"Of course! I'm happy you're here." Even if I'm internally freaking out. *What does this mean?* "I volunteered to help set up Holiday Lane, but we can drive to town if—"

"I don't want to mess up your plans. Let's do this together, then we can figure out what's next."

A man after my own heart.

I love volunteering in the community, creating opportunities for citizens to gather and bond. Wyatt's willingness to stay rather than feeling put out after traveling all this way to see me is a solid point in his favor.

Not that he needs more.

He's racked up quite the total these past few months with each letter and text message.

Three hours later, Holiday Lane is ready to open this weekend, and my friends are having way too much fun teasing me about Wyatt. The owner of the land and organizer of Holiday Lane, King Bishop, may have been suspicious of a stranger entering our volunteer group today, but his wife and my friend, Hannah, had no such compunction.

She and the wives of the Olson-Keller guys are having a field day.

"I can't believe you have two military pen pals!" Nora giggles, fanning her face in exaggeration. "Do Chris and Wyatt know about each other?"

"Wyatt knows about Chris; that's how we got to talking. But Chris doesn't know about Wyatt. I wasn't sure how to bring it up. Plus, I haven't heard from him since that first letter, so his opinion doesn't matter anyway."

"True." Hannah nods. "Wyatt didn't ghost you, and he showed up in town to surprise you—not to mention his help today. I'm sure he wasn't expecting to haul lighted reindeer around all day."

Probably not.

But he's been a good sport. Jawing with the men, being respectful and considerate of the women.

We're all laughing when my back spasms, freezing me in place. My face scrunches in pain as I grab onto the tree trunk by my side.

"You okay?"

Shaking my head, I breathe through the pain. "No... my back decided to protest today's physical labor." *Despite my attempts to leave the heavy lifting to the guys.*

Apparently, my body doesn't care for traipsing through the forest for long periods of time either.

"Shit. Let me grab Wyatt. Do you trust him to drive you home, or do you want one of us to do it?" Hannah asks, concern radiating from her eyes.

"I trust Wyatt," I mutter.

Readjusting my position causes another pain to shoot from my lower back, and embarrassment floods to the surface. My back problems aren't necessarily a secret from my close friends, but I hate experiencing symptoms in front of an audience, especially Wyatt.

I'm still relatively young, yet it feels like I'm decades beyond my age due to freaking genetics.

Wyatt jogs to a stop in front of me. The wind ruffles his short brown hair and plasters his flannel shirt to his broad chest and shoulders. He stripped off his heavy coat earlier once he started working up a sweat with the other guys, and my friends used the opportunity to rib me mercilessly about him losing layers of clothing.

Ugh! Why does he have to be so handsome when I'm feeling ninety years old?

"Hey! Hannah said you need a ride home. Are you okay?"

"I will be," I say, forcing the barest lift of my mouth into a smile. "I just need a break." Along with a pain relief tablet I should have taken earlier to offset my current circumstances.

"Are you sure?" His amber eyes narrow on my white-knuckled grip on the tree. "She didn't say what, but it's obvious something is wrong."

Licking my lips, I straighten slowly from my slightly hunched position. "I'll explain on the way to my place, but it's nothing serious. Trust me."

Wyatt doesn't seem convinced, his sharp jaw working like he's swallowing another question, but he matches the slow strides to my car without a word.

Each step requires immense effort, but it's my only option unless I want to sleep in the forest tonight.

"We can come back for your rental later. Sorry for the inconvenience." A wince pinches my cheeks as I settle into the passenger seat of my sedan. It's going to be hell standing back up.

"Forget about it. I'm not worried about that; I'm worried about you. What's wrong?" Wyatt types my address into his phone for directions.

Does he have it memorized from our letters?

That's sweet, even if I can't fully appreciate the gesture while sitting here in pain.

A short explanation about the hernia and scoliosis diagnosis follows, and as much as it sucks, at least there's an official medical reason for my back issues. For the longest time, I chalked it up to being overweight. Guilt ate at me for not exercising more or drastically changing my diet to alleviate my health issues.

Then my GP noticed how uneven my shoulders were, sent me to get some X-rays done, and what do you know? I have a fucking degenerative muscle disease. Would exercising more have helped? Sure, but would it have solved all of my issues?

Nope.

A silver lining amidst the storm of medical jargon.

"I wish you would have said something," Wyatt says as my apartment comes into view. "I could've helped more."

"How? You were already doing as much as possible. I'm not an invalid. Small spurts of manual work are doable, but I can't always predict how my body will respond. Don't blame yourself for not doing more. It's my problem, not yours."

Wyatt grumbles under his breath, and I bite my lip to hide a grin.

Let him disagree.

All that matters to me is how much he cares. Which, judging by his constant checking in and his desire to ease my pain, is a lot.

After parking, he rounds the car and opens the door, offering a hand to help me stand.

"Fair warning, this might take a minute." Mentally preparing myself for the lightning strike of debilitating pain, I carefully maneuver my legs to drape sideways over the seat, then after accepting Wyatt's hand, I push upward, biting my tongue to hold in a groan.

"Lean on me. I've got you."

Did I say there was a silver lining?

Because any positives are eclipsed by my current situation. Wyatt is a strong and capable military veteran, while I'm the woman with extra fluff and a bad back.

This has dark storm clouds written all over it.

"Thanks," I murmur, directing my eyes to the ground, self-conscious about needing his help to walk to my own apartment.

It's slow and torturous, but finally, we get inside, and a breath of relief deflates my lungs.

"Does laying down help? I can massage the area if you want."

Wyatt's hands on me? A thrill of nervous excitement bubbles to life. It doesn't matter if his touch will be more professional than romantic.

Wyatt's large callused hands will be on *me*.

"Let me take some medicine, then we can try a massage. I've wondered if it would help while I'm in this state, but booking an impromptu appointment with a therapist seemed like too much work."

"Well, I'm here now," he states matter of factly. Like he's not going anywhere.

But he means until Christmas, right?

Not forever?

CHAPTER NINE

WYATT

While massaging Kennedy's back isn't how I imagined my first time touching her, it doesn't detract from the pleasure I feel by making her feel better. I just wish she'd felt comfortable enough to share about her health issues before today.

Finding Kennedy braced by that tree in the woods—her body tense and pale despite the chill in the air—had kicked my protective instincts into overdrive. *What was wrong? How could I help?* Every inch of me vibrated with the need to relieve her pain.

A soft hiss pierces the quiet, and immediately, I pause my ministrations. "Is this helping at all?"

We decided that it might be better if she sat backward in a dining chair, so she could rest her arms on the headrest while I massaged her tense muscles. That way she wasn't alone in her bedroom with essentially a stranger.

I'd like to get there eventually, but this makes more sense when we only met a few hours ago.

"I think so," she says sleepily. Her head lays cradled between her folded arms, her dark lashes fluttering against her cheeks.

"Good." I've never given a woman a massage before, so it's a relief to learn I'm not total shit at it. I want to take away Kennedy's pain as much as possible.

"So… Did you come home with Chris? Someone mentioned that he's back for the holidays."

Her simple question holds a ton of weight; the implications clear. Is this a brief interlude before I return to hang out with my army buddy? Does Chris know about our friendship?

"No, we traveled separately," I say. Kennedy inhales a sharp breath as my fingers hit a tight knot, and I gentle my touch, wordlessly apologizing for the spasm of pain. "The truth is I came to Suitor's Crossing for you. Chris didn't factor into the decision."

"Oh."

Oh.

Is that concern I'm some sort of stalker? Or is she pleased by the admission?

Fuck trying to figure it out myself.

"Is that a good or bad *oh*?"

"Good." Kennedy stretches her arms overhead then cautiously rises from the chair as I step back to give her room. She carefully palpates her lower back before twisting to the side and flashing a shy smile. "I'm glad you're here, and I'm extra happy that we don't have to work around Chris or his family's schedule to spend time together. Don't get me wrong, his mom Sheree is nice, but it's going to be awkward when she finds out her machinations failed because we connected instead."

"I never would have had a chance if Chris took the time to write back to you," I point out, still pissed on Kennedy's behalf. She didn't deserve the way he treated her.

"Maybe, but it doesn't matter—" Firm pounding on the front door interrupts us, and Kennedy frowns at the sudden intrusion. "Who...?"

"Kennedy Elaine! Open the damn door!" An annoyed male voice booms through the hardwood, and instantly, I'm in defense mode, pushing past Kennedy to answer the demanding summons first.

Two men stand tall and bristling with anger on her doorstep. One is a firefighter based on the logo on his tee and the heavy turnout pants held up by navy suspenders. The other is harder to categorize in his tailored suit, though it's obvious the men are related—twins with their matching steel grey eyes and black hair, despite the firefighter's shaggier appearance.

"Who the hell are you?" the firefighter asks, his gaze bouncing between me and Kennedy, whose warm presence heats my back.

Placing a hand on the doorframe to block her from edging forward, I level a challenging glare his way. I don't know who these guys are, but no one gets away with banging down my girl's door and acting like a couple of overbearing dicks.

"Major Wyatt Lincoln, and you are?"

"Kennedy's brothers, Beckett and Ezra Caldwell." The suited man gestures to the firefighter then to himself. "We heard a stranger randomly showed up at Holiday Lane then drove our vulnerable sister home, despite a swath of friends present to take care of her. So, why don't you explain what the fuck you want with Kennedy?"

"Oh my god." Kennedy groans behind me. "Ezra, Beckett, calm down. Wyatt is a friend, not a stranger. Come inside before the neighbors start filming the show you two dummies are putting on. Who even called you guys?"

She tugs on the back of my shirt, and reluctantly, I lower my arm to let the men pass the threshold. One of Kennedy's letters mentioned that she has four older brothers. The reality of what that means is becoming clear—four overprotective men intent on forming a solid barrier between Kennedy and any man who dares to be near her.

As someone who views Kennedy as a precious treasure, I appreciate the sentiment, but their bullying won't work on me. They're not going to intimidate me into leaving my girl. No fucking way.

"King Bishop, and it's a good thing he did," Beckett says. "It's not smart to be alone in your home with a stranger, Ken. Anything could happen."

"I told you. Wyatt isn't a stranger. We've been writing letters to each other for months."

"Letters? Like the ones you're supposed to be writing to Chris Dugan?" Ezra sighs and runs a hand through his short hair. The disheveled look elevates the resemblance to his twin. "Fuck. How many men are you talking to?"

"Watch it," I growl, disliking the insinuation in his voice.

"One. Chris never responded to my letters after the first."

"So Major Lincoln decided to step into his place," Beckett scoffs.

"It's none of your business how we met. All you need to know is that Wyatt is here and he doesn't deserve to be treated like a criminal. King shouldn't have gotten involved. It wasn't his place."

"He's our friend and he knows to look out for you."

"I can look out for myself." Kennedy glances out her kitchen window and nods toward the red fire truck parked on the street. "If that's all, you should probably get going. Fires aren't going to put themselves out, Beckett. And the lodge can't last long without you, isn't that right, Ezra?"

Right on cue, a loud honk blares from the fire engine as a walkie-talkie crackles to life. Beckett turns down the volume before pinning both of us with a harsh glare. "This conversation isn't over. We'll have dinner tonight as a family to discuss things."

Kennedy rolls her eyes. "Whatever. Text me the time and place. *Not* Grandpa's. He doesn't need to be part of this."

"Agreed." Ezra nods. The brothers finally head toward the front door, but he pauses to glower back at me. "You fuck with our sister, you fuck with us. So be careful, Major Lincoln."

"Understood."

They leave with the soft snick of the door closing, and Kennedy gingerly sits on her couch with a groan. "I'm sorry about them. They take their brotherly roles way too seriously."

"That's a good thing. It means they care, and I can respect that. I'll just have to earn their trust like I have to earn yours." I sit next to her on the beige cushion, thankful when she doesn't scoot further away.

"You have mine."

"Do I?"

"Of course." A shy smile tugs on her plump lips, tempting me to taste their blush-pink sweetness. Only years of learned restraint stop me from acting on the urge.

Clearing my throat, I force myself to look away from her pretty mouth and mumble a garbled, "Good," before snagging the remote beside my arm and flipping on the television for a distraction.

"Want to watch one of your holiday movies before tonight's dinner? It might make you feel better considering how stressful today's already been." *And maybe it will help cool the desire hardening my cock.* Kennedy's not ready for that, so the damn thing needs to stop trying to punch a hole through my jeans before she notices it.

She watches the couple currently on the screen and silently asks for the remote with her outstretched hand. "This is a good one to let run in the background. You traveled all this way. I'd rather catch up."

So that's how we spend the rest of the afternoon relaxing on her couch. It's cozy and downright domestic and I wouldn't trade it for the world.

There's something warm and comfortable about chatting in front of the TV like this is a routine occurrence—exchanging mundane details about our days while unwinding at home.

"You're done?" Kennedy asks in disbelief.

"Yep, I'm officially retired at thirty-eight."

"But what's next?"

I shrug. "I don't know yet. There's a nest egg I've been saving for years, so I have time to figure it out."

She hums in her throat, understanding softening her blue eyes.

"Ready to tell me more about your brothers?" Changing the subject seems like the smart thing to do since I don't want her to dwell on the fact that I'm currently unemployed. She doesn't need to worry about my future because I'll always make sure I'm able to take care of her. "Does Ezra work at the lodge, too? You said something about him needing to be there?"

A pink flush rises on her cheeks, and she swipes a strand of hair behind her ear. "Uh, yeah, about that... My family actually owns the lodge." My eyes widen at the admission. "We're the third generation to run it. Ezra handles the day-to-day management, while I work on the event coordinating, and Soren, our eldest brother, is kind of the jack-of-all-trades, handyman-slash-groundskeeper along with Griffen."

"Wow..."

"I'm sorry I didn't share before."

"No, it's okay. I'm guessing that makes your family pretty important to Suitor's Crossing," I venture, brows lifting in question.

"Yeah, we're one of the founding families." She bites her lip and peers up through thick lashes.

"Really? Small-town royalty, huh, princess?" I tease, though a part of me balks at the knowledge. Why the fuck would a girl like her—a woman rooted in this town for generations, who is probably beloved by everyone—want to tie herself to me? A floundering loner with connections to no place and no one?

"My brothers maybe, but..." Kennedy hesitates. "The perks of being part of a founding family never really affected me."

"Why not?"

"Well, you saw Beckett and Ezra. They were one of two sets of twins at school and football stars. They were regularly voted homecoming king. Prom king. There was always a contest between the two of them. Soren was more introverted, but he led our debate team to three championships, which should sound nerdy but was actually amazing. Griffin is like me. More reserved, and not part of the popular crowd like our siblings. But he's a whiz at tech. Everyone goes to him for their random questions."

"And you were left unnoticed? What a shame. They missed out on an amazing woman," I murmur, shuffling closer.

I don't like the resigned shadow on Kennedy's face. Like she somehow failed to measure up to everyone's standards.

Because that's a bunch of bullshit.

Our faces near each other—a chance to steal the kiss I've been craving, an opportunity to erase that disheartened expression from her beautiful face.

Slowly, my lips press softly to hers then retreat. "Is this okay?" I ask, caressing her bottom lip with my thumb.

"Yes..." Her fingers sink into my shirt as she sighs into my mouth, giving me access to the sweetness within. The coy strokes of her tongue against mine tease and entice, and I groan with each tentative exploration.

I squeeze her lush thigh and hike her leg over my lap, so she's half-straddling me, and use my other hand to angle her head for deeper penetration. This woman is mine. All of her soft curves, and unique quirks—they belong to me.

For as long as she'll have me.

CHAPTER TEN

KENNEDY

T he Ole Aces has had a glow-up since Austin took ownership. He replaced the scuffed bartop with a gleaming new one that accentuates the rustic wood and metal light fixtures made by Suitor's Crossing's local blacksmith, Rhys.

Since Austin's upgrades, the bar is constantly crowded—a local hotspot for friends and family to hang out.

My brothers commandeer two tables and shove them together to form a mega section big enough for the four behemoths, Wyatt—a giant in his own right—and myself. Ezra and Beckett still look disgruntled after the afternoon's ambush, but now Soren and Griffen have joined them to voice their displeasure at my secret relationship.

Is it any wonder I kept it under wraps with these theatrics?

"When were you planning on telling us about him, Ken?" Soren asks, crossing his arms over his chest. He dropped his daughter off at Grandpa's before he and Griffen made the drive here to interrogate me, and I wish my niece were here as a buffer. At eleven years old, Sara Beth can hold her own against my brothers—they're firmly wrapped around her finger—and they'd temper their sour dispositions with a kid around.

"When I had something concrete to share, Sor," I mimic his grumpy demeanor with a raised brow.

Wyatt shields a cough of amusement then covers my hand with his, causing my brothers to stare at the gesture with varying degrees of suspicion. God, why do they have to be so distrustful? Is it so crazy to believe that an attractive military veteran like Wyatt could be interested in me?

"We weren't hiding our relationship," he says. "I'm not ashamed to admit my feelings for your sister." Wyatt's firm announcement elicits a rush of butterflies in my belly. "But this is the first time we've met in person. You'll forgive us if we want some privacy to figure things out before opening ourselves up to the opinions of others."

Ezra harrumphs, slouching back in his seat as two waitresses dole out our meals. With plates of steaming food in front of us, the next few minutes are blissfully quiet except for the occasional grunt of approval for The Ole Aces's simple but delicious fare.

As our dinners slowly disappear, another round of questioning begins, but this time I let Wyatt field the inquiries and revel in his patient but stout defense of me and my decision to keep my brothers out of our relationship for the time being.

Soren, Ezra, Beckett, and Griffen have always had my back.

Growing up as the youngest child and the only girl, I had my own company of knights in shining armor to fight my battles—whether it was Harry Gaston in the third grade after he stole my Power Rangers lunch box or the slick car salesman when I went to buy my first car at eighteen.

They've always formed a staunch protective line, but having Wyatt pick up the mantle and stand between me and my brothers' wrath is something altogether different.

Maybe it's because he's *choosing* to protect me.

He's not obligated by family ties.

Instead, Wyatt wants to step into the fray that is the Caldwell siblings because he cares. He *desires* me. The memory of our earlier kiss swoops in, and I chug my water to cool off. *The rough texture of his beard, the spearmint on his tongue...* I'd rather be back in that moment than placating my overbearing brothers.

He wants to protect me, not because he views me as his weak little sister, but because I'm his woman.

Or at least, I hope that's where this is all leading.

Because I want to be his. Not just for the holidays.

For forever.

THE POOL AREA IS EMPTY at this time of night as I lead Wyatt to the enormous outdoor hot tub that overlooks the back of the lodge. Trees form a sea of black that leads into the mountains rising majestically into the night sky—the perfect setting for a romantic midnight rendezvous.

"Are you sure it's alright to be here? I don't want you to get in trouble."

"We'll be fine. Employees get special privileges; family owners even more so." Though I doubt my brothers would appreciate me taking advantage of lodge perks to get laid.

But I couldn't care less about their feelings after the inquisition Wyatt and I endured at dinner. The moment we were free to leave I suggested returning to the lodge to relax after we picked up his rental. And what better way to unwind than a sexy dip in the jacuzzi?

Once we're at the stone steps leading down into the large tub, Wyatt grabs the back of his sweatshirt and pulls it over his head to reveal thick slabs of muscle from his chest, abs, and the enticing vee leading to the bulge in the swim trunks picked up in the gift shop.

"Everything okay?" he asks with a smirk, spying my cartoon-like jaw drop.

"F-fine..." I stutter and turn to shed the light layers I threw on top of my bathing suit. The vintage style highlights my breasts and hips. High-waisted bottoms suck in my belly while the slightly cropped top exposes a strip of skin around the smallest part of my middle.

When I bought it, I felt sexy—a modern-day pinup girl—but this is the first time I've worn it, and now I'm faced with Wyatt's toned physique, which has insecurities roaring to the forefront.

"To be clear, I don't expect anything tonight. The hot water will be good for your back, and we can relax and talk. That's it."

My heart melts a little more under his warm, understanding expression, especially with his consideration for my back pain, but I want more than an evening of chitchat. We've done enough of that tonight by braving my brothers' questioning.

Gathering my courage and shoving body insecurities down deep, I adjust the dial to start the jets and recline on the bench across from Wyatt. The sturdy bra cups of the bathing suit push my breasts high to gently bob in the water, and it doesn't escape my notice how fixated his gaze is on the sight.

"Thank you for saying that." My voice is huskier than usual. "But I'm expecting more tonight."

He wades into the water, the bubbles bursting against his abdomen, and a different kind of heat blooms between my thighs.

"How much more?" His voice is low and gravelly, barely audible over the roar of the jets.

"As much as you'll give me," I admit, then tentatively unhook the halter strap around my neck to let the ends fall. The bra cups remain on my chest, but the implication is obvious—finish the job, strip me, *fuck me*.

CHAPTER ELEVEN

WYATT

Fuck-me eyes. That's what Kennedy's stormy blue irises are communicating, and damn if I don't want to heed their plea.

After an evening of easing her brothers' concerns—as much as could be done during one meal—I wasn't sure how Kennedy felt about us, despite that scorching hot kiss.

I said a lot of things at dinner. Admitted to a strong connection. Voiced my commitment. They were all true statements, but I would have preferred to share them with Kennedy in private to get her reaction versus announcing it to practically her entire family.

"I want to give you everything," I rasp, sinking deeper into the bubbling water to cage her against the tub's stone wall.

Floating closer, I brush my mouth over hers. Gently. Tenderly. Then claim it in one possessive swoop, clasping the back of her neck with my hand and dragging her nearer.

Kennedy moans and scrambles for purchase on my slick skin as I fold her top down to release her heavy tits. The round globes tremble in the splashing water, and my mouth immediately drops to capture a pink nipple, sucking the enlarged tip deep.

"Wyatt!" Kennedy arches upward, shoving more of her soft flesh into my face, and I'd happily drown surrounded by her thick curves.

"That's right. Scream my name, baby." Who cares if we disrupt lodge guests? They're the last thing on my mind.

I work her bathing suit bottoms down her legs as I switch breasts, ensuring my girl's berry-sweet nipples receive equal attention as she writhes in my arms like a gorgeous sea nymph—all glistening curves and sexy moans.

Releasing her tit, I lick up her chest and neck to whisper in her mouth. "Turn around, baby. It's time to put these jets to work."

"W-what...?"

I twirl a dazed Kennedy to face the mountains and the powerful jet of water shooting from the jacuzzi wall. "I'm going to fuck you now. My dick in this tight little pussy and this jet teasing your clit."

My fingers part her slick folds to allow the stream of water to pound her clit unhindered, and Kennedy jumps in shock.

"Easy, baby." There's a bit of distance between us and the wall since I don't want the strong jet to hurt her, but even with the space, it's powerful enough to bring Kennedy close to climax as she wiggles to avoid the direct contact.

"It's too much. Wyatt... I can't..."

"Yes, you can. Should I give you something else as a distraction?" With one hand holding her pussy open, the other frees my aching cock and lines it up to her clenching hole.

The warm jet bubbles slide across my dick, but those aren't the heat I crave. I need Kennedy's hot cunt wrapped around my thick length, sucking the seed from my heavy balls.

"Please... please..."

I'm not sure if she's pleading for me to stop or continue. The sharp pain of her nails on my forearms could go either way. Pushing me back or pulling me closer.

With the head of my cock wedged at her entrance, I angle her head to the side so I can meet her glazed eyes.

"Do you want me to fuck you, Kennedy? Do you need me to stretch your virgin pussy with my big dick?" She'd shyly shared how innocent she was over a text chain months ago, and maybe it makes me a barbarian, but I love that I'm the first man she trusts to touch her.

Hopefully, I'll be the only man.

"Yes!"

"Say it," I growl. "I need to hear you say it out loud."

Kennedy bites her lip, a wave of self-consciousness inserting itself before her hesitancy clears, and she sighs. "Please, Wyatt, fuck me. I need you to—"

The slam of my cock forward cuts off the rest of her sentence.

CHAPTER TWELVE

KENNEDY

I've fantasized about hot tub sex. I live in a small mountain town, work at a luxury lodge, and have heard numerous stories from staff about finding couples canoodling all over the place. So, yeah, call it a bucket list item.

But experiencing the pleasurable burn of Wyatt's thick cock tunneling inside me while a continual stream of bubbles bursts over my clit?

Nothing could have prepared me for this.

"Wyatt..." I gasp, arching into his big hands as they strum across my body like a skilled guitarist, plucking my nipples and leaving goosebumps in their wake.

"Yeah, baby?" His teeth nibble on my earlobe. "Is this what you wanted? Is this what your needy little cunt craved? To be stuffed full of cock?"

Damn, he's got a dirty mouth.

His letters never hinted at this side of him, which is probably a good thing, since who knows how the military censors correspondence to ensure sensitive information doesn't get out? An entire room full of soldiers could have been privy to Wyatt's filthy words, something I'm loath to share.

My pussy clenches around his steel length, and I reach up to pull his head down to mine. "Stuffed full of *your* cock," I correct before pressing my mouth to his, eager to be claimed by every part of him—from lips and tongue to his rough fingertips and punishing cock.

"For such a good girl, you've got quite a mouth on you."

"Maybe I'm not so good."

He chuckles and hits a particularly sensitive spot inside with the blunt head of his dick.

"*Impossible.*" Suddenly, I'm lifted from the water, so my knees rest against the tub's stone edge, practically bent in half, and allowing Wyatt to slip deeper.

Holy fuck. I'm surrounded by him. His solid, muscular chest at my back. His flexing arms holding my legs open wider for his possession. Cool air sweeps over my clit, a stark contrast from the heat of the jacuzzi, and I shudder at the temperature change.

"Good girls let their man fuck them any way he wants to." Wyatt pinches my aching nipples. "Tits filling his palms. Cunt glistening for everyone to see. What would people say about the Princess of Suitor's Crossing taking cock like she was born to it, hmm?"

"Wyatt... Wyatt, please..." I'm begging, but I don't care. I'm so wired, so ready to *come*. It won't take much more to shatter all the tension he's built in my poor, sex-starved body.

Just one more filthy promise. One more delicious graze of his—

Stars explode behind my eyes as a strangled scream catches in my throat. Wyatt plunges deep to fuck me through the waves of my orgasm, and I swear I'm going to pass out from lack of oxygen... and an excess of pleasure.

"That's it, baby. Milk my dick... You're coming so well for me... My favorite girl." He nuzzles into my neck as my lungs fight for breath. I could happily float away and sleep for the next forty-eight hours. Except Wyatt hasn't finished yet.

"It's your turn," I mumble tiredly, tightening my core to hold his cock in place. My nails scratch down his side to grab his firm ass, tugging him closer.

"Don't worry about me. I'm not leaving this hot little pussy until it's painted with my seed," he growls. Instinctively, my body softens, bracing for his release, desperate to welcome the feral sign of his possession.

Another few thrusts of his hips and Wyatt groans. His cock jerks and swells, and our combined essence floods between my thighs in an obscene display.

"Fuck, baby... You sure know how to welcome a man home."

Offering a shy grin, I shrug, still cocooned within his warm embrace. "What can I say? I'm a hospitality expert."

A bark of laughter explodes from his chest, and we both end up laughing like two horny teens as we abandon the hot tub in favor of drying off and escaping to the room I reserved for us. The trip is lighthearted and playful, full of kisses in the elevator and the hallways.

And my heart pounds with a thrill of joy. Wyatt called Suitor's Crossing *home*. *Or he called* me *home*.

Either way, that's not the sentiment of a man planning on leaving anytime soon, right?

INSTRUMENTAL HYMNS welcome our family as we enter the church. The Christmas Eve service is a family tradition, and this year is even sweeter with the addition of Wyatt. While my brothers' ire has cooled a little since Wyatt's arrival two weeks ago, Gramps never had qualms and welcomed Wyatt into the family immediately.

Getting to know him these past few weeks without the barrier of an ocean between us has made this the best Christmas ever, yet my stomach turns at the possibility of seeing Sheree and Chris tonight. The past few Sundays I've missed the morning services to hang out with Wyatt, so tonight is the first chance that they might see us together.

Wyatt doesn't think Chris will care, and frankly, neither do I, but it'll be awkward running into Sheree after all she did to connect the two of us.

"Chin up, buttercup." Wyatt flicks my jaw with his finger. "No matter what happens, we've got each other."

"Laying it on thick aren't you, man?" Beckett grumbles from behind us.

"You would know," I tease.

Part of Beckett's bad boy allure is the way he flirts with women. He's a *love'em and leave'em* type, and most of the ladies around here don't mind, hoping they might be the one to change his M.O.

Soren and Gramps lead our pack with Sarah Beth between them, stopping to guide us into our normal pew towards the middle of the church. Unfortunately, this puts us right behind the Dugans who normally sit on the other side of the aisle.

"What are they doing here?"

Ezra shrugs, bringing up the rear of our group. "Hell if I know, maybe they heard you were bringing your man tonight. Isn't he Chris's commander or whatever?"

I don't have a chance to respond when Sheree ends her conversation with the woman beside her and faces us.

"Kennedy," she says imperiously. "What's this I hear about you dumping my Chris for one of his friends?" She crosses her arms over her heaving chest, ruffling the pearl necklace hanging around her neck.

"I didn't dump Chris," I gently correct. "We just didn't hit it off." I refrain from disparaging her son by adding he never responded to the rest of my letters.

"What else do you call it when I set you up with my boy, and instead you show up to a family Christmas Eve service with this stranger?" She gestures to Wyatt.

"Ma'am, I apologize for the surprise, but now is not the time. We're all here to celebrate the holiday and the birth of Jesus, right?" His brow rises.

"Don't patronize me, young man."

"Mom, what are you doing?" Chris appears finally, and I wonder if this is a good or a bad thing.

"Look at who's seated behind us."

"I can see, Mom." Chris offers a fist bump to Wyatt and rolls his eyes toward the ceiling where murals of clouds and angels reside. "Things weren't serious between me and Kennedy. If she and Major Lincoln hit it off, good for them."

"But—"

"No." Chris raises his hand to stop her rebuttal. "Come on, let's return to our usual seats. See you guys."

He ushers her out of the pew along with his silent father to their regular spot on the other side of the church, and I release a sigh of relief.

"Well, that was entertaining." Griffen smirks, sharing a look of amusement with my brothers.

"Shut up."

"Hey, we're in church. This is a religious service. Show some respect."

"Shut up, *please*," I drawl, causing all of us to crack up in laughter. The showdown with Sheree, and Chris's consequent approval of our relationship, seems to have thawed my brothers out as they loosen the sticks from their butts.

We hold our lit candles, sing carols, and listen to a retelling of the nativity as the children act out the scenes on the altar. By the time the service is over, snow is falling, creating a winter wonderland just in time for tomorrow morning.

"We expect you bright and early tomorrow," Grandpa says with a wink, patting Wyatt's shoulder and hugging me before leaving with Griffen. The rest of my brothers repeat the actions—pat Wyatt's shoulder, hug me goodbye. Then we're left alone in front of my car with giant snowflakes melting on our faces.

"How are you feeling?" he asks, cupping my red cheeks.

"Better now that we've gotten through that conversation with Sheree and Chris."

"I figured he'd be okay, and his mom will get over it soon enough. She's probably already got another woman lined up for him."

"God, I feel sorry for that poor girl." Chris doesn't seem interested in a relationship, which is all good and well, except his mom isn't getting the memo.

A Christmas carol floats on the air from the speakers that line Main Street, and it adds to the holiday atmosphere.

"Can you believe we're going to have a white Christmas? It's an early gift."

Wyatt holds the passenger door open for me. "Yeah, but I already got my present."

"Oh, really?"

"Yeah..." His eyes twinkle in the night. "*You.* Merry Christmas, baby." Then he presses a gentle kiss to my lips, stealing the goofy grin his answer brings.

I guess I got my Christmas present early, too—the man of my dreams.

My holiday *heart spark.*

EPILOGUE

WYATT

TWO YEARS LATER

"Don't stop... Don't..." Kennedy gasps as my lips purse around her clit and suck harder. Ever since we learned about her pregnancy, her sex drive has been off the charts—something I'm extremely willing to satisfy with my fingers, mouth, or cock.

I glance up and marvel at her round baby belly, though it sucks that her heavy tits are blocked from view. Her arms flex and I imagine her delicate fingers playing with the swollen nipples, tempting dribbles of milk to fall. Fuck, I can't wait to taste that creamy sweetness when the time comes.

Sure, it's nutrition for our baby, but it's also sexy as hell, and I'm not going to pass up an opportunity to devour my wife in all ways.

"Come on, baby," I command, rubbing my bearded cheeks in her honeyed cunt. "Once you come on my face, then I'll let you ride my dick." And I'll get the prime view of her bouncing breasts that I'm currently missing.

Damn, I'm a lucky bastard.

Every day, I marvel at my good fortune. The love of my life—my *heart spark*, according to town legend. A healthy baby on the way. And a family of brothers who accept me as their own now that I've proven my worth.

For all the shit I put up with in childhood—the instability, the loneliness—life made up for it by giving me the Caldwell family. Kennedy's letters found a man hungry for connection and dared him to reach for something he never thought possible.

Love. Affection. Community.

Pausing, I lift my head and meet Kennedy's lust-filled eyes. "I love you, baby."

Her gaze softens as she lowers a hand to cup my cheek. "I love you, too, and so does this baby. You're going to make a great daddy."

I drop a tender kiss on her abdomen, picturing our child safely swaddled inside, and feel a rush of emotion. The two most important people in my life are right here.

It's a privilege to be loved by them. To protect them.

And I will never take that for granted.

Ready for more Caldwells? Don't miss *Ezra the Billionaire* next!

THANKS FOR READING & DON'T FORGET TO RATE/ REVIEW!

Please consider leaving a rating/review. Ratings & reviews are the #1 way to support an indie author like me.
Also, don't miss out on free books and up-to-date release information. You can sign up for my newsletter here[1].
I appreciate your support!
XO, Hallie

---

1. https://www.thearrowedheart.com/hallie-bennett

ABOUT THE AUTHOR

Hallie prefers steamy, insta-love stories where curvy girls are claimed by filthy-talking heroes. And when she ran out of reading material, she decided to write her own stories. If you want a quick, hot read, she's your girl!